ALIEN ABDUCTION FOR PIRATES

THE INTERGALACTIC GUIDE TO HUMANS

BOOK 4

SKYE MACKINNON

Alien Abduction for Pirates

Cover by Peryton Covers.

Published by Peryton Press.

skyemackinnon.com

CONTENTS

LESSON 1

HOW TO BECOME A LECTURER

[1]

AEDAN

I stare down the barrel of the blaster and wish I could jump back in time. Only an hour would do. Change our course, evade the enforcer ships that have now surrounded us. Or a day into the past, when we took on a ship a lot bigger than us and underestimated the determination of their crew. They damaged our shields and long-range sensors, which is why we never saw the enforcers coming. Now it's too late.

"Pirate Aedan," their commander, a purple-skinned Lurian, snarls. His tusks curl out of his mouth, signalling his aggressiveness. Lurians are the perfect enforcers. Anti-social, emotionless, always angry. They produce the best weapons in the galaxy and have no qualms about using them.

"Captain," I correct him. "What's the reason for this?"

"Reason?" he spats. "You're a wanted criminal. I've been chasing you for months. Stretch out your arms."

I think of refusing, but I have no doubts that he's itching to shoot me. He'd get less pay for a dead target, but I don't think he cares. Lurians aren't driven by money. They're all about violence and their old-fashioned sense of justice. In their eyes, all pirates are scum.

I hold out my hands and he clamps magnetic shackles around them. They glow an ominous blue. I bet they have some kind of torture mechanism built in.

"You will tell your crew to surrender peacefully," the Lurian commands. "We will shoot anyone who resists."

I sigh and turn around to look at my crew. None of them looks happy to give in, but it's not like we have a choice. I refuse to get any of them killed.

"Don't resist," I tell them with a growl.

La-Layna, my second-in-command, flashes her fangs when they put the shackles on her, but brothers Len and Panan hold out their arms without showing any emotion. They move as one, like always, as if one is the other's shadow. They have a mental connection unlike anything I've ever come across. It's not typical for their species, but then, they're nothing like other Karangi. Their kind is known for their benevolence, yet here they are, part of my pirate crew.

They herd us into the belly of their ship and lock us into individual cells. The walls between them are translucent so I can see my friends, but the cells are completely soundproof. My own breathing is loud and distracting. I need to make plans. I've been caught before and I've always found a way out. This time won't be any different.

THE KARANGI JUDGE stares me down, her third eye unblinking and seeming to stare into my soul.

"Aedan Xerxi, you are-"

"Captain," I drawl.

"Your ship is not legally registered and you are therefore not worthy of the title," she says in her soft yet icy voice. "You are hereby sentenced to ten galaxy-standard years on the prison planet Y103. You will labour there every day of your sentence to make up for your wrongs."

I suck in a sharp breath. Ten standard years. That's fifteen Ferven years. By the time I get released, I'll be too old to sire offspring. Not that I have any plans of doing that, but it's something that highlights the length of my sentence. It's unusually harsh. We're pirates, but we try not to kill the crew of the ships we hijack. I always tell them that we're after their cargo, not their lives.

"What about my crew?" I ask hoarsely.

"Nine galaxy-standard years each unless you confess to coercing them. That will lower their sentence to five years each and will add another five to your own sentence."

"Don't do it," La-Layna whispers from my left. "We'll be fine."

"I'll take the fifteen years," I announce, ignoring her. "If you reduce their sentence to three."

The judge's third eye finally blinks as she stares at me. "You're not in a bargaining position. However, I appreciate your sentiment. Maybe I have to offer you a bargain after all."

Hope blossoms within my chest, rising all the way into the curled tips of my horns, but I keep my face impassive.

"What kind of bargain?"

"You've abducted aliens from other planets, am I right?"

I nod wordlessly.

"How many?"

"Twenty. Maybe more. We've not done a lot of abductions recently, our priorities have shifted."

"Then you may want to shift them back. The Intergalactic University is desperately looking for a new Alien Abduction teacher. Interest in their classes is at a record high and they lack tutors with real-life experience."

I try to hide my surprise but fail miserably. "You want me to teach at the IGU?"

"There will be a trial period. If you fail, you will be sent to Y103. If the Dean of Abductions is happy with your teaching, you will continue to work there until you retire at whatever age is customary for Ferven males."

I stare at her, trying to see if she's toying with me, dangling a treat in front of my nose only to pull it away when I reach for it.

"I'd need my crew," I tell her. "I can't conduct abductions without them."

"Naturally. They will be able to choose if they want to be your teaching assistants or if they want to apply to be teachers in their own right. The same rules apply. Work full-time until retirement."

"What about pay?"

"We shall start at a reduced rate of fifty per cent, that should be enough to cover food and accommodation without tempting you to return to a life of crime. Every year you work for the IGU, the salary will increase by ten per cent until you reach the full salary for a lecturer."

I mull her proposal over. No more pirating. No more daring escapes and dangerous hijacks. We'd have to go back to mundane life. Jobs. Regular hours. A tiny salary that won't pay for the luxuries we're used to. But we'd be free, almost. If we're sent to the prison planet, there's no way to know if we'll be able to escape. We might be stuck there for years.

I turn to Len and Panan. Their third eyes are closed, signalling that they're engaging in a mental conversation.

"I'm all for it," La-Layna mutters under her breath.

"Let's take her offer before she realises we have no idea how to teach."

I nod and wait for the brothers to open all three of their eyes. "What have you decided?"

"We agree," Panan says quietly. "This is the best option. Plus, we have some savings that we can use to supplement our income."

Len touches my shoulder and his voice fills my mind.

She never said we can't take a part-time job at the side. We have enough contacts to make some money, even without capturing ships.

He's right. We won't have to live in poverty like the judge intends. When you've been a pirate for as long as we have, you learn that wealth lurks everywhere, just waiting to be acquired by a shrewd pirate. Violence isn't always necessary.

I turn back to the judge. "We agree to your bargain with one condition: our ship remains ours. We're going to do our abductions on her and not some rust bucket the IGU provides us with."

The Karangi looks me straight in the eyes and once again I feel like she's staring right into my soul.

After what feels like a small eternity, she inclines her head. "I agree. Enforcers will take you to the main IGU campus where you will meet Professor Katila. My sister."

Ah. That explains things. She's not doing this out of the goodness of her heart, but because she's doing her sister a favour. Let's hope that Professor Katila is a little less stuck-up.

THE PROFESSOR's purple skin is a little paler than that of her judge sister, but their marbling pattern is exactly the same. She looks at us from her three eyes, studying each of us individually.

We arrived at the IGU campus station late last night, but the enforcers kept us locked up on their ship until it was time for our meeting. My back hurts from sleeping on the bare floor of my cell. I can't wait to be back on my own ship and in my fluffy, comfortable bed.

"You will need other clothes," Professor Katila announces. "You need to look the part. And we will have to install cameras on your ship to make sure your students can see every part of the abduction process. I've decided that before you get your own class to teach, you will show my current students what you're capable of. They will learn from both your success and your mistakes. I'm sending you to Peritus, or Earth, as the natives call it. They're a backwards species with only limited spaceflight capability. Don't underestimate them, however. They're graded as a difficult abduction objective in my curriculum, but I think you need a challenge to prove your worth."

"Cameras?" La-Layne snaps. "I won't be ogled around the clock."

Professor Katila sighs. "They will only transmit

once you're ready to start the abduction process. Personal living quarters will be exempt, although the room where your abductee will be kept has to be under observation for welfare purposes."

"We need control of the surveillance system," I say sternly in my most commanding Captain voice. "I don't want you spying on us. Full control."

The Karangi rolls her two lower eyes. "Trust me, I have better things to do than watching you all day."

LESSON 2

ABDUCTING A HUMAN IN NEED

[2]

MAY

I look down the cliff and my heart beats even faster. It's a long way down. My stomach quenches at the sight and I step back to get my breath back. I've been afraid of heights ever since I can remember. At one point, even the thought of standing this close to the edge of a sheer cliff would have given me an anxiety attack. Today though, it's different. I *want* to be here. I will only have to fight the fear a little longer.

The bottom of the valley calls to me. The stones are black, of volcanic origin, and barely covered by vegetation. They'll make a hard bed, but by the time I lie on them, I won't feel it anymore. I won't feel anything anymore. That's the purpose of all this. I want it all to stop. Life sucks and it's not kept any of its promises. There's nothing left for me.

My parents are dead. My fiancé is dead. My dreams are dead, too. My life no longer has a purpose and I see it for what it is: a waste. It's time to put an end to it.

The wind tousles my hair, pushing a few strands of my jet-black locks into my face. A storm is coming. The clouds above are racing across the sky, grey and foreboding. If I was here to hike, I'd seek shelter from the elements about now. But I'm not here on holiday.

I've left an envelope on my suitcase in the little bed and breakfast I checked into last night. Some money for the owner, as an apology for the inconvenience. An explanation that this was my choice, that I wasn't killed by someone else. And the key to my little flat back in Glasgow. I don't have any family left who could inherit my belongings, so I assume my landlord will simply throw them out and get a new tenant. One who always pays their bills on time, unlike me. I've been job hunting for so long that I can barely remember having a regular income.

I take a deep breath and step forward again until the tips of my walking boots are at the very edge of the cliff. The ground up here is muddy and the bottoms of my trousers are wet with dew and moor water. Scotland is a wet place, I realised that again today. I won't make it any wetter with tears. My eyes are dry. There's no point in crying. This is my choice.

I relax my body, pushing away all the stress of the moment. I want to be happy during the moment I die. I'm going to fly and I will feel true freedom.

With one last look at the beautiful yet broody sky, I walk into nothingness.

I fall.

Fall.

Fly.

And then I stop falling. Suddenly, the wind no longer kisses my face. All sound has vanished, as has any kind of movement. I'm hovering in the air, suspended by a force I can't see. Nor can I understand what's happening. Is this death? Have I already landed at the bottom of the cliff and this is just an echo? The beginning of the afterlife? I had really hoped there wouldn't be any such thing.

A strange, glaring light envelops me. It covers me from all sides, yet the sun is still hidden behind clouds. What the fuck...

I'm yanked up and I scream. For the first time today, I'm afraid.

As if someone put a rope around my waist, I'm pulled upwards, bum first, my arms and legs dangling. I struggle even though there's nothing to struggle against. Maybe I'm being sucked into hell. That would be just my luck. While there was no wind during that moment of stasis, it's now stronger than ever. My shirt rides up my belly and I wish I'd kept on my jacket. I try to reach for it and pull it down in the silly hope that clothes can protect me from whatever's happening, but I can't reach it with the wind fighting my every move. Instead, it's pushed up even more until it's around my neck like a scarf, exposing my entire front. And I'm not wearing a bra. I'd wanted to be comfortable during death and I've always hated wearing bras.

The world beneath me is quickly disappearing. The Cuillin mountains on the Isle of Skye, the place I'd selected as my final destination, now look as tiny as the fake mountains of my late grandpa's model railway. And still, I'm rising, pulled up relentlessly. I must be close to the clouds soon. It's freezing, but I'm not sure if I'm shivering because of the cold or fear. I'm finding it harder to breathe.

The moment I enter the first cloud, I close my eyes. I'm not sure I want to see any of what's about to happen. Angels jumping around on fluffy clouds. A gate leading to heaven, guarded by some saint with a large golden key. Virgins waiting to be deflowered.

What I get instead is a spaceship. There's no doubt that's what it is. The swirling metal that seems to move like quicksilver while I look at it, the way it hovers above the cloud without a sound, the light that vanishes into a circular hole in the middle of it. This is a textbook flying saucer and I'm the helpless human being abducted.

For some reason, I find it easier to believe in an alien abduction than in angels dancing on clouds. I've always hoped that there's *more* out there, not just our puny little planet that we're on the best track of destroying.

I am sucked into the spaceship, bum first, my breasts on full display. Not exactly the way I'd have imagined first contact. The force pulling me abates as soon as I'm inside a dark room. I get one last look down at the clouds below before the hatch closes, leaving me in complete darkness. I'm gently lowered to the floor. It's surprisingly warm, even though it feels like metal. The floor vibrates ever so softly, but I can't hear the sound of any engines.

Behind me, a door slides open with a barely audible whoosh and I stagger to my feet to face my abductors. I only see the alien's silhouette as he – she? – stands in the doorway. Behind them is bright light, similar but not quite as intense as the glaring light that enveloped me while I was sucked up through the air.

The figure is huge, at least seven feet tall. To my relief, they only have two arms and two legs. No tail, no extra limbs. They don't look like a squid or beast either. The only alien thing about them is their height and two large horns that curve from the sides of their head. Plus a decidedly purple skin colour, visible even against the light. For some strange reason, this gives me hope that I'm not here to be their dinner. That's completely irrational, I know that. They could be hostile, no matter the way they look.

Without warning, the room is drenched in light. I squeeze my eyes shut and cover them with my hands. It's too bright, like looking right at the sun.

"Why are you exposing your udders?" a booming voice – most definitely male – echoes through the room.

I think I'd prefer the angels after all.

LESSON 3

INTRODUCING YOURSELF TO YOUR HUMAN

[3]

AEDAN

The female presents her udders to me, proudly pushing out her chest. She must be in heat. Not quite what I was expecting, but I won't complain.

For a human, she's surprisingly attractive. She's tiny, yet voluptuous. Her hips are wide, promising that she'll be a good breeder. If I decide not to keep her, she'll fetch a good price on the black market. Not that I'd ever sell her as a slave. I'd persuade her to choose a male as her mate and then take the credits they'd usually pay for a slave. My last abductee found a wonderful home that way.

Done with the presentation of her assets – truly beautiful udders that I want to squeeze and nibble on – she pulls down her shirt before covering her face again with her hands. Is this some kind of courtship ritual? I've not been to Peritus before and Professor Katila didn't allow us much time for researching its inhabitants. At least she provided us with an update to our translator implants, allowing us to talk to the female in her language until she gets her own implant.

"Can you turn down the light a little?" she says. Her voice is musical, swinging up and down with every syllable. It's unlike my own monotonous accent that rarely changes pitch.

With a simple thought, I command the ship to dim the lights. Unlike the rest of the crew, the ship responds to my brainwaves. One of the reasons why I insisted that the IGU let me use it for abductions.

"Better?" I ask.

She slowly removes her hands, blinking rapidly. She nods, which I take as an affirmation. It's a strange fact that the majority of one-headed species across the universe use nods to mean 'yes'. Of course, there are exceptions, but it's always struck me as curious.

I look up at the camera attached to the ceiling to my right.

"The abductee has arrived safely. Now it's time for the introductory talk. Sometimes, I like to point a weapon at them to stop them from freaking out and trying to run away, but I don't think it's necessary with this female. She has already presented me with her udders, which I believe is a mating ritual in her culture. This is an excellent sign suggesting that she'll be open to future mating and breeding."

It feels silly talking to the camera, but Professor Katila has made multiple threats in case I don't act like a teacher. It's a small price to pay in exchange for mine and my crew's freedom.

"Breeding?" the female huffs. "You're not breeding with me, pal."

I grin at her and stroke one of my horns. There's a direct correlation between a Ferven's horn size and the length of his cock. Hopefully, this human knows that. Even if she doesn't, stroking my horns feels almost as good as stroking my cock. Seeing her full udders has affected me and I'm straining against the fabric of my tight trousers. They're boring, fashionable clothes that the IGU insisted I wear while being on camera. They want their teachers to look the part, so I had to exchange my pirate clothes for this lacklustre outfit.

"Welcome to my ship, human. I am Captain Aedan and I have abducted you. This is permissible according to paragraph seven-slash-fourteen of the Intergalactic Federation's Regulations because your planet has been designated as unimportant to galactic affairs. You are safe with us and we will not harm you, unless your species requires to be harmed for your wellbeing. Would you like some sustenance? Otherwise we shall begin the probing."

"Probing?" she gasps, a most adorable sound that makes me even harder. "Release me immediately or it will end badly for you."

Her bravado is betrayed by the slight trembling of her limbs and the widening of her eyes. Still, I admire her strength. None of my previous abductees have kept their composure like this.

"I have no intentions of releasing you, female. I abducted you, which gives me the right to tell you what to do. Before we proceed, what is your name?"

"You're not going to tell me what to do, pal. I demand that you return me to Earth and leave this planet."

I can't help but laugh. She's adorable, with her hands on her hips and an insolent look on her pretty face. Just like Ferven females, she has no horns, but her hair is a lot shorter than any female on my planet would ever wear it, only reaching to her shoulders.

"If you're not going to tell me your name, I shall choose one for you," I say sternly, trying to suppress my laughter. It's not a good look on camera to make fun of my abductee. "How about Silence? It's what I'd like from you just now."

"My name is May," she snaps. "What are you?"

"What? I should tell you that's very offensive, but I do forgive you because this must be your first contact with an alien species. Who. I'm a Ferven, one of the three dominant intelligent species on the planet Allopa. I have three crew members who you'll meet shortly. Len and Panan are on the bridge, while my first officer La-Layna is currently preparing the medbay for your probing."

She steps backwards without taking her eyes off me. Smart female.

"You're not going to probe me. No way. I don't know what kind of sicko you are, but you can stuff your probes into your own arse."

I chuckle. "Feisty, I like it. But you don't need to worry. The probing will be pleasurable for you and me."

"Fuck you!"

"I'm afraid that's not part of the probing, unless you really want to."

She retreats further until her back is pressed against the wall opposite. Well, she thinks it's a wall. It's actually a door, the door leading to the medbay. She's about to get even angrier.

I smirk and slowly walk towards her again. I'm herding her like an animal and while it should make me feel a little guilty, it actually turns me on.

"Captain?" Len's voice echoes through the room and I look up at the camera. We've rigged them so we can see what they're filming, not just the IGU people monitoring us.

"Yes? What's the problem?"

"We've got company. You better come and look."

I turn back to May. "It seems your probing has been postponed. Follow me."

"No thanks, I'd rather stay here."

"Suit yourself. It's going to get very cold in here in a moment though. We don't want your cargo to melt."

"Cargo?"

She looks around the empty room.

"We had to move it into another area of the ship while we were getting ready for your abduction. It wouldn't have looked good on camera if you'd arrived in a room full of crates. So they say."

May points at the camera. "Why are you filming this?"

"If you want to know, you'll have to come with me. I'm needed on the bridge and don't have time to stay here for any longer."

I turn and stride out of the room, smirking when I hear her follow me. She's feisty, but she's clever enough to go along with my demands for now. I have no doubt though that she'll rebel again as soon as she gets the chance.

Now that I'm no longer distracted by her looks, I realise the urgency of the situation and walk a little faster. We didn't expect anyone else in this part of space. Peritus has a few satellites circling it, but nothing worth mentioning. Other abductors? That's pretty much the only reason why anyone would come to Peritus, save for conquering their planet, and that would go against Intergalactic Law.

Everyone's assembled on the bridge, including La-Layna who was supposed to be busy with preparing for May's probing.

"What's going on?" I demand.

Len pulls up the greenlight scanner on the main screen. It shows two blinking dots that are quickly approaching our location.

"Two vessels, they're refusing to identify themselves. I've scanned their subwave signal, they're not pirates. They're still too far to analyse what kind of ships they are, but I estimate they're small. Scouts, maybe."

All pirates who know what's good for them use a subwave signal embedded in all communications to avoid pirates hijacking other pirates. It still happens, on purpose, but it avoids a lot of trouble.

"Are they coming to rescue me?" May asks from behind me.

La-Layna laughs. "Human, no one on your planet knows we've taken you. And in space, nobody cares. Besides, we abducted you as part of an IGU course. It's all official."

"IGU?"

"Intergalactic University," I explain. "Now shush."

“A university told you to abduct me?” she explodes. “Am I going to be their lab rat? An exhibit in their museum? Are they going to dissect me?”

Instead of fear, I only sense anger from her. Curious. Until now, this was just a thing I did to keep my freedom. A filmed abduction, one of many to come. But seeing her glaring at her fate in this way, clearly ready to fight, makes my cock hard with desire and my heart filled with pride. How peculiar, pride for a stranger. And not just that, an abductee who's under my control, who's not much better than a slave at this point in time.

“Shut up,” Panan hisses. “We have bigger problems. They just put up their shields. Strong ones. Our weapons will barely able to make a dent if it comes to it.”

“Shields up,” I command, trying to push May from

my mind even though she's standing right behind me. "Red alert."

The bridge is drenched in pink light. I keep telling Len to fix our lights to make them red again, but he either doesn't care or his memory is worse than I thought. Maybe he just likes garish pink.

"It looks like we're in a brothel," May mutters from behind me. "Please tell me I'm not going to be your sex slave."

"You won't," I say absentmindedly while studying the screen. "Any response yet?"

"Negative," La-Layna reports. "They're staying silent. Do you want me to start an evasive manoeuvre?"

"No. I want to know what they're doing here."

"So do I." Professor Katila's voice booms through the room and her face appears on a screen to my right. Figures that she's watching us.

"Do you think they mean you any harm?"

I turn to her. "We don't know yet. It could be a coincidence that they're here at the same time as us."

"That's a rather major coincidence."

"Agreed. Are any of your students planning missions to Peritus?"

"Yes, but none of the current class are advanced enough yet to attempt an abduction. Two of my best students, A-Ven and A-Vay, will conduct their final assignment here later this term, but I had them in my tutor group just now, so it's certainly not them."

La-Layna clears her throat. "Captain, they're hailing us."

"Put them through."

"It's voice only, no video," she says quietly before a crackling interrupts her.

"Enemy ship, get out of our way," a female voice snarls.

My translator implant does its job, but I would have recognised that harsh accent anywhere. Pletorians. The scum of the galaxy. Not honourable enough to be pirates, too violent to integrate into galactic society, too stupid to realise that. They're scavengers, taking on other species' technology because they're too dumb to develop their own. They must have stolen the ships they're on. There's no way a Pletorian could have an advanced shield like this.

"What are your intentions here?" I demand.

Before they can answer, May does the most stupid thing she could have done.

She shouts "Help!" at the top of her lungs.

I've abducted an idiot.

LESSON 4

HOW TO KEEP YOUR HUMAN FROM MAKING MISTAKES

[4]

MAY

I don't understand what the aliens from the other ship are saying – only the four aliens around me are speaking English – but they're my only chance of rescue. I refuse to be probed, dissected and turned into a museum exhibit. It can't get any worse than this, can it?

Aedan stares at me in anger. His horns seem to bulge from his skull, making him even more intimidating. I shrink away from him, just in case he decides that he wants to do the dissecting before the probing after all. Not long ago, back on Earth, I wanted to die. Now, I have a fierce desire to live. In one piece, without probes, with my body intact, with my freedom unbroken.

The alien from the other ship growls something which makes the four beings around me spring into action. They push buttons, type stuff into their holographic keyboards, and Aedan suddenly wraps an arm around me and pulls me against him.

Obviously, I struggle. Especially when something hard pokes against my back. Please let that not be what I think it is.

"Stop," he hisses. "They might try to beam you over, but they can't while you're touching me."

He's just given me even an even better reason to get away from him. The enemies of my enemies are my friends, right? Aedan and his crew are kidnappers, so the other aliens must be better than that. Maybe they can fly me back down to Earth.

I pause at that thought. Do I even want to go back?

It doesn't matter. I certainly don't want to stay here waiting to be probed. I ram my elbows into Aedan's chest as hard as I can. He groans, but his grip on me only tightens.

"They're Pletorians, you idiot. They'll rape you, beat you, sell you as a slave."

He could be lying, but the slight panic in his voice tells me otherwise. Fuck. From the frying pan into the fire. That hadn't been my intention.

I stop struggling and press closer against him. I don't want to be beamed to the other alien ship after all. I don't even mind Aedan's hard cock against my back. I wonder what it looks like. Will it be human or more...alien? Does he have more than one, maybe? Or is this not a dick but something else entirely? For all I know, his species could reproduce asexually. He might grow a little Aedan somewhere on his body, like in hydra corals. It's not like I have any clue about aliens. Humans might be the only species that has sex in the entire universe. His cock - well, his hard appendage - jerks against me and I hope to all the Gods that I'm wrong.

"You cannot have her," he says loudly while protectively crushing me against his chest. It feels strangely good. It shouldn't, but it does. "I abducted her. She's mine."

"Stealing an abductee would be a serious breach of Intergalactic Law," the female alien on the screen adds. I don't know if she's talking in English or if her voice is somehow translated, but at least I can understand her, unlike the aliens on the other ship. Just like the two males on the bridge, the female has three eyes. It should look strange, but they somehow suit the shape of her skull. The eye in the centre of her forehead is wide open and doesn't blink, while the other two could almost pass for human. Her purple skin is paler than that of Aedan and has a beautiful marbled effect, with patterns swirling all over her face and neck. She reminds me a bit of one of my tutors at the Royal Conservatoire - stunning but incredibly stern. An ice queen.

"You are being watched," she continues. "I am ready to send ships after you should you not retreat at once."

"This isn't your remit," Aedan hisses. "I abducted her, I'm going to protect her. We don't need your help."

The female rolls her third eye in exasperation, but doesn't say anything more.

The aliens reply in harsh, guttural words that make a shiver run down my back. They don't sound happy. And somehow, I doubt they'll simply back down.

"What are they saying?" I whisper.

One of the two three-eyed males in front of me presses a button and suddenly the harsh sounds turn into English words.

"...claimed her. Surrender her or be prepared to be obliviated."

"I'm not going to give her to you. She's *my* human. Mine."

The way he says that makes me clench my thighs together. Goosebumps erupt all over my arms. The way he said that... *Mine.* I've never heard anything this sexy before. It's like an orgasm embedded in a single syllable. *Mine.* I want him to say it again.

"Our ships are stronger than yours. We'll blast you into atoms." The Pletorian sounds thrilled at the prospect. I wait for Aedan to deny that fact, to say that we outgun them, but he stays quiet. Which means we're screwed. And all because I couldn't keep my mouth shut. But then, I was abducted today. I deserve some lenience.

"Delta-four manoeuvre?" the female on the bridge, one with yellow skin and fangs that look like they could easily rip a chunk out of me, asks in a whisper.

"Do it," Aedan commands. "May, prepare yourself. This might be a little uncomfortable."

With no further warning, the galaxy expands right inside my stomach, tearing me apart.

I RESURFACE to the sounds of my own retching.

"I only cleaned here yesterday!"

I blink open my eyes and stare at the puddle of vomit at my feet. I'm still in Aedan's arms. Wow. He never let go of me even when I started puking.

"Your human is going to clean that herself," the yellow female complains. "I don't know if the cleanbots can deal with human body fluids."

"Are you alright?" Aedan asks softly. His breath is hot against my neck.

I nod and immediately regret it when the room starts spinning.

I groan. "What did you do?"

"A series of evasive manoeuvres followed by a fusion jump. It takes a while to get used to those. I'm sorry I didn't have the time to prepare you for it."

"Is that like a warp jump?" I ask weakly.

"Warp? What's that?"

Seems Star Trek was just fiction after all.

“We've got away from the Pletorians and Professor Katila has informed the Intergalactic Authority. They'll send some ships to make sure those scum don't attack Earth.”

“Is that like the police?”

“Yes. They're under the control of the IC, the

Intergalactic Council, which in turn is made up of representatives of all the planets signed up to the Intergalactic Accords."

"You seem to really like that word, Intergalactic. What happened to the Federation?"

He stares at me blankly. "I've never heard of that."

Figures. Definite proof that aliens have missed out on the joys that is watching Star Trek. I pity them.

"We should start the probing now," the female interrupts. "We should give her a check-up anyway. Who knows how the fusion jump affected her fragile body."

Aedan nods and stands up, me still in his arms.

"Oi, let me down, you big pink ram!"

He chuckles and ignores my demand. "I assume *ram* isn't a compliment."

"It's an animal found on Peritus," the yellow female explains. She presses a button and a large, unflattering picture of a ram appears on the screen. Its wool is dirty and its eyes lack all intelligence.

"Nice horns," Aedan says, true appreciation swinging in his voice. "I had no idea you had such gorgeous creatures on your planet. Maybe we should go back and get one. Are they kept as pets?"

He turns around and the movement makes my stomach lurch. I barely manage to keep myself from puking, but I decide it's better to keep my mouth shut for now. I close my eyes, hoping that will stop the room from spinning.

"Let's get you to the medbay," Aedan says softly.

"La-Layna can give you something to make you feel better."

"Only if she promises to clean up the mess she made," the female hisses.

"Be nice, Lay. You know this abduction has to go well..."

I want to ask why, but I don't dare open my mouth.

Aedan carries me through the ship and even though I'm curious about what it all looks like, I keep my eyes shut. The nausea is getting worse rather than better. I think Aedan is trying to be as gentle as possible, but it's still too much movement for me. I just want to lie in my comfy bed back home and sleep.

Finally, he lowers me onto a soft mattress. I'd assumed I'd end up on a cold metal table in their medbay, overlooked by scary machinery. Instead, when I slowly blink open my eyes, I'm in a friendly-looking room with walls in pastel colours and several lights above me shaped like planets. No weird probes anywhere. Phew. That's reassuring.

La-Layna, the yellow alien with the fangs, has followed us and is now rummaging in cupboards that look like they'd be more at home in a country house kitchen rather than a spaceship. Without a word, she takes something that looks like a small sanitary pad and places it on my forehead. It's warm, almost hot. I try to reach for it, but Aedan captures my hands in his.

"It'll help with the nausea," he explains. "Just let it do its work."

The strange pad seems to be melting, becoming

sticky and wet. I really want to wipe it off, but the male isn't releasing my hands. His skin is rough yet soft at the same time. No idea how that works. It feels good.

"Nice," I mutter. "You feel so nice."

"Trust me, I'll make you feel much better. Soon. After we've mated, you'll never want another male again."

"Mate," I whisper and smile. "That sounds good. Mate me. Now."

His horns seem to swell and his grip tightens. "Don't tempt me, little human."

"I think she's having a reaction to the patch," La-Layna says sharply. Her voice doesn't fit the pastel all around us. "I'm going to take it off."

She wipes my forehead with something wet and cold. I moan in protest. I want to keep feeling like this. Happy and content and very turned on. All that talk about mating has left me wet.

"Is she ready for the probing?" Aedan asks and I squirm a little.

Yes, I'm ready. So ready.

"Give her a moment. I'm not sure if her arousal is due to the drugs or natural."

"Natural, obviously. Have you seen me?" Aedan replies cockily.

I squirm a little. *Cocky*. I want to see his cock in all its glory. I have no doubt that he's going to be...delicious.

"Wait," La-Layna advises. "I don't think it would

look good if we take advantage of her while she's in this state."

"Take advantage of me," I beg. "Probe me, now."

The female wipes my forehead again, as if to make sure all of the patch has been removed. I grab her hand and hold it tight, marvelling at how soft she feels.

"Touch me, please," I moan and look at her.

She exposes her fangs, but her lips are curved into a half-smile. Or maybe it's a fearsome battle grimace. Not that I care. Aedan will protect me. Then probe me. Then fuck me.

LESSON 5

STAYING IN CONTROL DURING PROBING

[5]

AEDAN

I can smell her arousal. It's spicy, tangy almost, and makes my cock push against my trousers. If I could, I'd tear off my clothes and ram into her, fucking her without restraint. But I'm not that kind of man. Besides, she's still under the influence of the patch La-Layna put on her. I don't want to take advantage of whatever strange brain fog she's under just now.

I look up at the camera. The light's blinking, meaning we're being filmed. No surprise there. I better get on with the probing before Professor Katila decides to intervene.

La-Layna must think the same. She's taken out her Diagnoser and is scanning my human from top to toe. If she has toes. Large boots cover her feet. Curious, I remove them and the fabric sleeves she's pulled over her feet. Not sure why she needs those. Maybe she can't afford well-fitting boots.

She has five toes, cute and round. I run a finger over them, feeling her soft skin.

"That tickles," she protests. "Do you have some kind of foot fetish?"

"Just checking how many toes you have. Part of the probing."

La-Layna snorts but doesn't say anything.

"Is she healthy?" I ask my second-in-command.

"I'm going to give her an antidote, just in case," La-Layna announces and jabs something into her neck.

May shrieks in surprise and I glare at my second-in-command.

"You could have been gentler," I admonish her.

La-Layne rolls her eyes. "Now everything's back to normal, according to the Diagnoser. We can proceed with the probing. Do you want to undress her or shall I use the Liqu ı fier™?"

I grin. "I'll undress her. We wouldn't want to risk harming her."

I know exactly that there's no way the Liqu ı fier™ could hurt the female, but I need an excuse. I want to slowly strip off her clothes, revealing her body to me. I've already seen her udders, but that was from a distance and not the same as it will be once she's bared in front of me.

She doesn't protest when I open the button of her fabric trousers and gently pull them down along with the flimsy undergarments she wears beneath. In fact, she lifts her hips to make it easier for me. Again, I marvel at how wide her hips are. Perfect for breeding. She'll be able to carry many offspring for me, maybe even several at once. Multiples are rare in Ferven females, but they have a different anatomy from my little human.

I get even harder when I think of spilling my seed into her, creating new life. I'm close to coming and she's not even touched me yet.

Her legs are smooth and her dark skin shimmers under the lights of the planet lamps above. Those were my idea. When I saw them at a space station, I couldn't resist, even though they were more expensive than I would have liked.

I run my hands down her calves, relishing the softness of her skin. She's exquisite.

"Hurry up, I don't have all day," La-Layna complains. She holds a probe in her hands, glaring at me with impatience. I don't know what's wrong with her. She's been cranky ever since we abducted the human. Is she jealous?

"You don't have to stay, I can do the probing," I tell her sharply. "I've read through the files and watched some vids. I know what to do."

The Kardarian gives me a doubtful look. "Are you sure you're going to get scientific results and not just relief for your cock?"

"Out, now."

La-Layna shrugs and leaves the room. I'm alone with the human now. She looks at me with wide eyes, but I don't think it's because she's scared of me. Not anymore. She's aroused. She wants this.

I spread her legs and she makes a tiny little sound, a moan that makes me harder than ever. Her pussy glistens with moisture. I won't need any lubricant for the probe. I take the metal probe and warm it in my hands. I don't want it to be uncomfortable for the little human.

"What are you doing?" she asks hoarsely.

"I'm going to insert this probe into you and explore what you look and feel like from inside. I will need to know what kind of alien cocks you're compatible with. Plus I want to make sure you're healthy. The probe also collects other data that will be sent to the university's database and added to the files about humans."

"Alien cocks?" She sounds like there's something stuck in her throat. Maybe I should probe her there, too.

"If you want to be bred, you need to know which alien is safe to be with you. You wouldn't want to be torn apart. I can already see how tight you are, even with all your wetness."

"I'm not wet," she protests.

Without thinking, I dip a finger into her. She's just as warm and tight as I imagined. She doesn't protest. No, she actually wiggles her hips as if she's encouraging me to continue.

My cock strains against my trousers. I want to plunge into her depths, fuck her hard. But we're not alone. We're being filmed and I'm supposed to probe her, not fuck her. I had no idea being an abductor was this hard.

I pull out my finger and hold it up to show her. "Look, you're lubricating."

Again, she does a choking sound. "That's not what you call it."

I shrug and begin to insert the probe. It slides in without opposition. It's almost as if her pussy greedily sucks it in. Data appears on the screen, together with an image of her rosy tunnel. It takes all my self-control to continue with the probing and not take her here and now.

She gasps when I push the probe in a little further. I still don't meet with any resistance so I continue until the probe bumps against an obstacle. I check how deep it is. Good, she'll accommodate my cock. Nothing stands in the way of our mating. Yes, I mentioned her being with other aliens, but that was just a formality. Now that I've seen what she's hiding beneath her clothes, I know she's mine. Not just because of her body. I like her mind, too. And her scent. And the softness of her skin. And...

The probe beeps, signalling that all the measurements have been taken. I leave it in for a moment longer and enjoy how sexy the little human looks with her legs spread apart, wetness dripping from her swollen pussy, and my hand with the probe in the very centre of it all.

"Can you turn off that beeping?" May asks.

I hadn't even realised the probe was still making a noise. I was too focused on her wet pussy.

I switch off the probe and put it back in its casing to be cleaned. I almost lick off her juices myself, but we're being filmed and that wouldn't look very professional at all. Looking back at the female, I realise she's still wearing her shirt. That simply won't do.

"I'm going to remove your shirt so I can measure the circumference of your udders," I announce, pretending to be in possession of my wits. I'm not. I doubt I'll be able to touch her beautiful udders without doing something stupid, like rubbing my throbbing cock against them. It was the first thing I saw of her, back when she arrived on the ship. Two perfect mounds, begging to be squeezed.

"Breasts," she says.

"What?"

"They're called breasts, not udders. Or boobs. Tits. Knockers. But definitely not udders."

"I apologise," I reply and I realise I mean it. I don't want to offend her, even though she's only my little abductee. Not that her udd...breasts are little. "It must be a fault in translation."

She shrugs and sits up a little. "I guess that makes sense. I'm impressed by how well this translation is working."

I leave my place between her legs - I shall return! - and slide up her shirt, exposing her gorgeous breasts.

"Breasts." I enunciate the word carefully, letting it slide over my tongue. "Breasts."

May laughs, surprising me. Should an abductee be laughing during probing? I highly doubt it. I'm making a mess of things. Time to behave professionally and get this over with before I end up with a wet patch on my trousers.

I take the Diagnoser and hold it above her right breast, letting it do its thing. It's safer than using a manual way of measuring them. I doubt I could stop once I start touching her.

Once I've got full measurements of both breasts, I step back. "That's the probing done," I announce with relief. "Unless you'd like some anal probing while we're at it?"

"Shouldn't you be touching me?" she asks with an evil smile. "I don't think that gadget can quite estimate the hardness of my nipples."

"Hardness?" I repeat hoarsely.

And I was doing so well...

A switch flicks within me and all control dissipates. I press against the bed and place my hands on her breasts. It's like they were made to be squeezed by me. They're the perfect size, not too small yet not so big that I couldn't get a proper hold on them. Her nipples are hard against my palms and I decide to conduct a scientific study on them. How long will they stretch if I pull on them? I experiment first with the left, then the right. I don't really remember the results, too distracted by May's moans and whimpers.

She seems to enjoy me playing with her nipples.

Maybe it's like with my horns. When they get stroked, it's almost as if someone's stroking my cock. In the name of science, I should find out. With one last gentle squeeze, I let go of her udd...breasts and focus on her pussy once more. She never closed her legs. Yet another sign she's enjoying this. Drops of her lubrication have run onto the sheet.

Slowly, I circle her opening with one finger, relishing in her moans. They're slightly louder than when I was massaging her breasts. Does that mean they're not connected? Or are they?

I'm a lousy prober. Not that I care.

I stare at her pussy and do the only thing that makes sense. I pick her up, swing her over my shoulder and run to my cabin as fast as I can.

As SOON AS the door closes behind us, I push her against the wall, rip down my trousers and enter her with one hard stroke. She gasps, clinging to me for support as I start to fuck her the way I've wanted for way too long. She wraps her legs around my hips, letting me push even deeper. Her lips are half parted as she breathes heavily and I can't help but press mine to hers, kissing her. She returns the kiss immediately, her tongue swiping against mine. She's showing me that she's willing and eager.

I set a fast pace, knowing I won't last long, not after the torture of probing her. I should get an award for my restraint. But now there's no holding back. We rise together, travelling as fast as starlight, our bodies conjoined, our breaths as one.

LESSON 6

LEARNING HOW TO SELF-EVALUATE

[6]

MAY

I wake up in the arms of an alien and it feels fantastic. I'm slightly sore, but it's a good kind of soreness, reminding me of all we did together. After the probing, Aedan took me to his cabin and introduced me to the most amazing bed ever. It reminds me of a waterbed on Earth, shifting beneath me with every movement, but it also supports me in all the right places. I'm convinced it changed temperature too, keeping us cool while we were creating our own heat and then warming me when the room's cold air conditioning woke me up. There's no blanket, but I don't know if that's Aedan's preference or if blankets and duvets are a human thing. If I'm to stay here, I will certainly demand one. Even if the bed keeps me warm, I need something to snuggle under. Right now though, I've got an alien to snuggle with.

Aedan's eyes are closed and his breathing is slow. He looks even more gorgeous when asleep. Not having a blanket means his entire body is on display. His *naked* body. I resist the temptation to run my hands over his chest. His ten-pack would make any human male wild with jealousy. And let's not even talk about his cock. Even now that he's sleeping, his cock is half-erect and looks ready to plunge into my depths. I wonder if he's having a sexy dream or if this is normal for him. I need to learn more about Aedan, about Fervens.

But will I? For that, I'll have to stay.

I pretend I have a choice. If he asked me, would I want to go back to Earth? Or would I want to leave him at the next space station, forging my own destiny in the universe?

I turn away from Aedan and look up at the ceiling. His beauty is distracting me. Especially his horns. They make me want to touch them whenever my gaze falls on them. It's like they're calling to me. I shake my head. What a silly thought.

Back on Earth - or Peritus, as the aliens call it - I was ready to end it all. Now, I've been given a chance of a new life. I can start from the beginning again. Make new friends, explore new places, find somewhere to call home. I can reinvent myself. Get rid of all the things I didn't like about me and create a new May. I could call myself June.

It was a running joke in my family. If I did something wrong, my mum would say that June would know better in future. If I succeeded at something, she'd praise how much better I was than April.

Now, I could become June for real. A new me, risen from the ashes, with no past and a wide-open future. All the possibilities.

But I'm being too optimistic. Just because I'm no longer on my home planet doesn't mean that my depression will just vanish. I've had it since I was a teenager. There are good months and bad months, good days and bad days. Most people have no idea how much I suffer until I do something stupid like jumping off a cliff. It wasn't the first time I'd tried to end my life. As much as I want to believe that my new surroundings will heal me, I have to be realistic. Especially now that I don't have my meds. I've not thought of that until now. They didn't always help, not as much as I wanted them to, but I think they did make a difference. Maybe the aliens have an antidepressant that's more effective. Maybe they even have a way to cure depression. But do I really want to tell them about it? I'm not sure if there's a stigma about it here like there is on Earth. I only ever confided in my best friends and my family. My fiancé knew, but I didn't tell him right away. At work, nobody was aware of my issues.

"Go back to sleep," Aedan mutters groggily.

"How did you know I'm awake?"

"My horns are tingling. You're thinking too hard."

"Your horns?" I turn onto my side and give him a

quizzical look. "Don't tell me you can read my thoughts."

"No, sadly I can't. I'd love to know what you think about last night."

I smile at him. "You only have to ask."

With a tired groan, he turns to me and his golden eyes sparkle with mirth. "Did you enjoy the probing?"

"Surprisingly, I did. But I liked what followed even more."

"I don't think I can remember. Maybe you should show me? It might jog my memory."

A chuckle escapes me. "That's a pretty good pick-up line."

"I don't need to pick you up. You're already in my bed. And you're going to stay here, little human, until I've ravished you again and again."

Heat pools between my legs. I flick my gaze at his cock and swallow hard when I see how much he's grown already. Yes, I'm sore, but that won't stop me. I've never had better sex than with him and I'm going to take full advantage of that. Who knows how long it'll last. If I leave, I'll at least have the memory of how amazing sex can be. That's the beautiful thing about memories. You can take them with you wherever you go, relive them, savour them as often as you like. Sadly, too often the bad memories prevail, pushing away the good ones.

"Why are my horns tingling again? What are you worried about?"

"What exactly can your horns do?" I retort with no intention of answering his question.

Aedan sighs. "They can detect tension and worry in others. Only when I'm close, though, like I am with you now. Not every Ferven can do that. Yet another reason why I'm special."

He winks at me, suddenly looking very human. If you ignore his purple skin, golden eyes, curled horns, oversized cock and ten-pack. Basically, he looks human if you squint, unfocus your eyes and tip your head sideways.

"Now tell me what's wrong," he says softly. It's not a demand, it's a gentle encouragement. I think he genuinely cares. But that's too early, right? I was abducted only a day ago. Crazy how much longer it feels. Like an eternity.

"I don't know what to do," I reply after a moment. It's a vague answer, but it's all I can say for now. I don't want to reveal too much. I don't even know this male. I've explored his body, but his mind is still a mystery.

"I'd suggest you could kiss my cock again like you did last night, but I don't think that's what you're talking about." He grows serious and his eyes turn darker, like pools of molten gold. I could drown in those eyes. "Are you worried about what happens next? About how you'll fit in as my mate?"

"I'm not your mate," I say automatically.

"Maybe not now, but you will be. I don't have the slightest doubt about that. When I look at you, I see a kindred spirit. You may be a strange alien from a backwater planet, but you're resonating with me. I can feel it in my horns. We're made for each other, little human, and nothing in the universe can keep us apart."

A pleasant shiver runs down my back. He's serious. He really thinks we're meant to be together. I wish I could let go of my doubts and simply believe that. But that's not me.

"For now, we're going to continue with the lessons the IGU has mandated. Professor Katila has given me a list of what we need to do and-"

I sit up straight, staring at him in shock. "Did they film us?" I ask with a strangely squeaky voice. "Did they watch us?"

I'd really like a blanket now to hide under until the end of time.

He gently takes my hand and pulls me back down. "No, they didn't. There are no cameras in my cabin. They did record the probing, but I adjusted the camera angles before we abducted you. They mostly saw my back."

I look at him, a strange warmth surrounding my heart. He didn't have to do that, yet he did. He protected me from the cold, exposing eyes of the cameras.

"Thank you," I half-whisper.

"Even if I hadn't done it then, I would now. I get angry at the very thought of them watching us. Seeing your naked body. I want to be the only male who gets to gaze at your beauty."

"That's not your decision to make. You don't own me."

Aedan inclines his head. "You are right. It's the other way round. You own *me*."

AEDAN

I want to say so much more to her, but Professor Katila's voice interrupts my train of thought. While she has no cameras in my room, she does have access to the intercom.

"I have some feedback to share with you about the probing," she says without a greeting. "And since this will be great content for the course, I need you to go to a room with a camera. Now. Bring the abductee. I have questions for her."

I glare at the empty space in front of me, wishing I could tell that annoying Karangi what I think of her interruption.

"What does she have on you?" May asks. "Why do you let her command you around?"

"It was this or ten galaxy-standard years on a prison planet. I thought it was the easier option. Now I'm not so sure." I grimace and slide off the bed. "I'd invite you to the bathroom to get clean, but I doubt the Professor will grant us that time. Later, I promise. I want to worship your body from top to bottom."

Her eyes widen at my words and her pupils dilate.

It pleases me how much she reacts to me. It's clear that she craves me as much as I do her. I want to bury myself in her tight wetness again, mate with her, claim her, but it will have to wait.

She follows me off the bed, but she looks lost and unsure.

"What's wrong?" I ask.

"I don't have anything to wear. My clothes are still where you probed me."

"I keep forgetting that you're not from a modern civilisation. If we had time, I'd let you choose an outfit from the fabricator, but for now, the Magic Wand™ will have to do."

She snorts. "Magic wand? I don't think you mean the same kind of wand I'm thinking about." Her eyes flick to my cock and I'm instantly desperate to know what wand she means. But again, no time. Curse that unfeeling three-eyed academic.

I pull the device from a drawer and show it to her. "The Magic Wand™ is the opposite of the Liquifier™. Same company. It creates matter from seemingly nothing, although I know that's not true. I'm not techy enough to understand how it does what it does, but luckily it's very easy to operate." I point it at her and immediately, black fabric begins to form around her body. It covers her like a second skin, showing off her curves and udders. Her nipples are hard beneath the new garment, inviting me to pull and twirl them like I did last night. My cock twitches at the memory of the sounds she made...

"That's handy," she says, twisting to see herself from all sides. Maybe she's checking if I left some well-placed holes in the fabric. If it was just the two of us, I may have. I like teasing my females. From now on, there will be only one female. May.

Instead of using the Magic Wand™ on myself, I quickly put on some existing clothes. The trousers are nice and loose, hiding my erection. I'm not sure how I'm ever going to get any work done in May's presence. She oozes sensuality.

I turn away, very aware that if I keep staring at her, we'll end up back in bed. As much as I would like that, I know better than to keep Professor Katila waiting.

I lead May to the command room. It barely deserves that name. It's a glorified cupboard, but because it's next door to the bridge, we're pretending our ship is bigger than it actually is and have called it the command room. The screen already shows the Karangi teacher, her three eyes fixed on something we can't see. At least she's not glaring at us like she so often did during our initial training.

"Finally," she says without looking up. "Let's start with the abductee. Human female, how would you rate the probing?"

May exchanges a look with me. I give her what I hope is a reassuring smile. Of course, I want her to declare that it was the most amazing thing she's ever felt, but I don't want to influence her rating. I don't think that would look good in front of the Professor.

"I've never been probed before, so I don't have

anything to compare it with," she says after a moment. "But I think he did everything the right way."

I deflate a little. That's not exactly high praise.

"Did you enjoy it?" Professor Katila enquires.

My little human squirms a little, then nods. "I did. So yes, I give him five stars. It was amazing. At first, I was scared, but then Aedan made me feel safe. I enjoyed every second of the probing and don't you dare judge me for it."

She glares at the Karangi. I want to reach out to her and show her how much I appreciate her words, but I stay still and pretend to be all business.

Professor Katila turns her attention to me. "I agree with your abductee's assessment. It was a well-done procedure. Of course, there were a few things that could be improved upon, but in general, it will be a good case study for my lessons. However, what I'm more interested in is your mating afterwards. It's normal for abductors to get a little carried away during probing and turn it into intercourse, but you went further than that. You took her to your room and continued your mating there. For hours."

I freeze. How does she know about that? There are no cameras in my cabin. Did one of my crew tell her?

May looks at me with anger and betrayal sparkling in her brown eyes. "You told me no one was watching us," she hisses under her breath.

The Professor laughs. "You didn't think we'd actually agree to miss out on all that data? Yes, there are no cameras, but we did install sensors and microphones in all the rooms. Even without the mics we would have been able to know that you spent hours copulating."

I snarl at her. My horns itch with the need to attack her and avenge my mate. If she was here in the room with us, there'd be no holding back. There's a reason why Fervens aren't known for their patience.

She holds up a slender hand. "Hear me out. Listening to your mating has given me an idea that you might find agreeable."

I grip the edges of my seat to stop me from tearing at the screen and wait for her to continue. May shoots me a worried look but also stays quiet.

"There has been an increased interest in humans recently," Professor Katila begins. "More and more of my students want to travel to Peritus, while many of my staff have also registered their academic interest. I've realised we don't have enough data on humans. Yes, we have a few case studies of how to abduct them, but we're missing information on what happens after. Their mating behaviour. Their reproductive cycle. Their raising techniques for offspring. Their social interactions. You get the picture. We're going to send a research mission to Peritus, but that will take some time. So, I have come up with a way to gather more data in the quickest way possible. You."

LESSON 7

HOW TO BE A ~~PIRATE~~ Trader!

[7]

MAY

"Me?" Aedan and I ask at the same time.

The three-eyed alien turns to me, gives me something resembling a smile - although there's no warmth in it - and then looks at Aedan.

"You. The two of you are the perfect couple, especially because we've filmed your progress from the very start. Now we can see how your relationship progresses, how quickly you will lay eggs, how-"

"Humans don't lay eggs," I interrupt her rudely. "And that's a no from me. I'm not going to be your lab rat. No more filming."

"I'm afraid that's not your choice." She doesn't sound apologetic in the slightest. "You're the abductee which means you're at the very bottom of the decision ladder. I'm the one who says what's happening. This isn't a question, it's me informing you about the next step."

"No," Aedan growls. "You're not going to do this to us. We can continue as planned, completing the rest of your lessons, then I can abduct the next person, while May will stay my mate, off-camera. Mine alone. You can find someone else to do your dirty work."

"Dirty work?" she repeats, her centre eye blinking rapidly. "I've not asked you to dissect the human, have I? That would be dirty... but also highly illegal. Stop your complaining, can't you see I'm giving you the best possible option? Instead of having to abduct again and again, this could be your ticket to an almost normal life. You can become traders again, travelling across the universe, with your little human by your side. All we ask in return is regular full reports, biological data, maybe weekly psychological evaluations. I'll still have to discuss with my colleagues what exactly we need on a regular basis."

"Traders?" I whisper to Aedan when the alien stops for a moment. "I thought you were pirates?"

"She's being politically correct. And I highly doubt she's going to let us go back to that. But-"

"Because I'd hate to have an unmotivated teacher among my staff, I will give you a standard hour to decide. Just be aware that if you continue to abduct females, you are expected to probe them just as intensely as you probed your human."

I want to growl at her. I'm not letting Aedan put his

fingers into other women's pussies. Only mine. Aedan is mine.

I gasp at my own feral thoughts. When did that happen? Is this some kind of effect of space radiation messing with my mind? I've been abducted. I've known this guy for a day. He's probed me. And yet every fibre of my body wants to touch him. I crave him like a drug. Worse. Like a mate.

"We'll call you back," Aedan says brusquely and switches off the screen. He rubs one of his horns, clearly unhappy with the situation.

"I'm sorry," he sighs. "I don't think there's much I can do. She may call me a teacher, part of her staff, but in the end, I'm no more than a slave. She has full control over me. If I don't do what she commands, I'll end up on a prison planet and you - I don't know what would happen to you. I doubt they'd let my crew take you back to Earth. Best case, they'd bring you to the IGU station to learn more about humans. Worst case, they experiment on you. I won't let that happen." He jumps off his chair and pulls me up, right into his arms. He squeezes me against his chest, so tight I can barely breathe. Not that I mind. He's warm, he's hard, he's safe.

I must be completely brainwashed. Maybe space radiation is messing with me. How is it that I'm not scared?

The only fear in my mind is about having to leave him. I'm not afraid of him at all. It's messed up. Stockholm Syndrome for the win.

Aedan puts a finger under my chin and forces me to look into his golden eyes. His lips, almost the same mesmerising colour as his lips, are slightly parted as if he's about to speak yet can't find the words. I simply look at him, at this beautiful alien. His horns, so masculine and feral. His purple skin, alien yet gorgeous. He swept me off my planet and brought me to the stars.

I don't want to leave him.

"Let's do it," I whisper. "We'll be together. Maybe we can figure out a way to get some concessions. If they want us to be their lab rats, they better provide us with treats to make us perform."

"Are you sure?" he asks, his voice ever so gentle. "I don't want them to invade our privacy like that. I swear to you, I never intended to... this wasn't supposed to..." He swallows hard and looks me straight in the eyes. "I didn't think I'd fall for you. It was just a job. Abduct a human, go through the motions, drop her off, abduct the next one. All I wanted was to have my freedom. Mine and that of my crew. I never thought the female I'd abduct would end up my mate. But you are. You're my mate. I can feel it in my horns. The bond is still growing, but soon, even the suggestion of someone taking you from me will make me kill them. Fervens are highly territorial, I should warn you of that. You'll be the only female I'll ever touch again, but in return, I expect you to be mine forever. Even now, my horns ache at the thought of other males around you. And knowing some might watch us..." He growls. "I can't. I still have myself under control, but once we've mated a few more times, I'll tear this ship apart on the search for hidden cameras. It's impossible. I-"

I shush him with my lips. I kiss him, soaking in his worries, hoping to ease them. I don't have a solution, but I can't stand to see his pain. I reach up and cup his face, holding him in place just in case he gets other ideas. He's not the only one who can be possessive. He groans against my mouth and then he takes over, plunging his tongue into my mouth, devouring me. We're drowning in each other, clinging together, hoping for a future that might be impossible.

"Very nice."

Professor Katila's voice makes me step back in shock. I'm breathing hard, both from the kiss and from searing hot anger that's boiling up in me.

"Listen," I snap at the screen where she's appeared again. "I may not be a Kaji-... Kajaj-... Ka-"

"Karangi," Aedan whispers.

"Whatever, but I have rights. You can't just take away all my privacy. I'm not a criminal. I've been taken from my planet against my will, surely that counts for something?"

"You-" she starts, but I don't let her continue.

I channel my best Lady Macbeth in the performance of my life. A failed actor I may be, but I can do *angry* if I want to. Oh yes.

"My turn," I snarl, glaring at her in my best evil witch impression. "You're going to let Aedan and me be together. You won't force him to abduct other females.

You'll let him work as a trader again. In return, I promise to answer any questions you have about humans. I agree to regular medical tests as long as they're painless and not invasive. No constant filming. No invasion of our privacy. Deal?"

She stares at me with all three eyes wide open. None of them blinks for at least half a minute while she sits still as a statue, processing what I've just said.

Aedan reaches out and squeezes my hand. I don't turn to look at him, instead keeping my gaze on the enemy.

"We will keep the sensors to monitor your biodata, but we will remove the cameras and microphones in all but a few rooms. Twice weekly interviews with you about human biology, psychology and sociology. Weekly reports from you, Aedan. And if you conceive offspring, we will switch to daily reports and measurements."

"Non-invasive," I insist immediately.

Professor Katila looks like she's bitten in the sourest apple ever. "Agreed. Aedan, you will no longer receive a salary from the IGU. We will reimburse your human for her time, but consider your effort part of your punishment. You will be able to trade and travel where you want to, but any sign of illegal activity and our agreement will be null and void. You'll be sent to prison planet Y103 and the human will be mine to study."

Aedan nods grudgingly. "No pirating. Got it."

"I'll draw up a contract. Until then, the cameras stay."

The screen goes black, but both of us wait a moment longer, just in case she's still listening. I don't like that woman. She enjoys being in charge way too much. She's a manipulative bitch who needs to be put in her place.

Aedan wraps his arms around me and pulls me against his chest. "You were magnificent. Truly magnificent."

"You think so?"

"You'd make an amazing pirate. Not that we're pirates." He chuckles. "We'll be well-behaved traders. Boring, but better than the alternative."

"I wouldn't call travelling through space boring. Are we going to visit other planets?"

"Unless you want to stick to just space stations. We could go to Epsyl-4, one of my favourite places in the galaxy. The mountains are made of diamonds and sparkle in the light of their four suns. We can have a picnic in one of their meadows. They have fluffy little animals there that will come for cuddles. Not shy at all. I've always wanted to take one of them home, but an adorable pet doesn't fit my mean, grim pirate image."

I laugh. "It can be my pet and you can borrow it from time to time."

"Deal. It's a date."

"A date?"

"I read about those when preparing to abduct you. It sounded like a fun tradition that I'd like to try. Would you like a date on Epsyl-4, my little mate?"

I look up at him, butterflies bouncing up and down

in my stomach while heat embraces my heart. Instead of a response, I stand on my tiptoes and kiss him.

THE GRASS SMELLS of chocolate and cinnamon. I breathe in deep, almost tasting the cocoa on my tongue.

I'm on another planet.

I still can't believe it. I jump up and down a little, elated at how different the gravity feels. Everything here is different. The light breeze carries sounds that I can't identify. They could be made by plants or animals or the diamond mountains - I have no idea. My only reference points are what I know from Earth, but those aren't enough. I lack the words to describe this place.

Creatures as large as blue whales float high above us, reminding me of airships. They make weird trumpeting noises as they float among the clouds. The ground beneath my feet is soft, almost like jelly, but it solidifies when you step on it. Again, it's hard to put it into words.

"Come join me," Aedan calls and I force myself to look away from the air whales. My purple alien has prepared an actual picnic for us. A blanket, various tubs containing food and even a bottle of the strong liquor he calls Blastwater. I can only take a shot glass of that stuff, anything more makes me dizzy. And horny. Probably exactly what Aedan is hoping for. The blanket is big enough for us to lie on... if the date progresses well.

Not that I have any doubts about that. It's taken us a week to get to Epsyl-4 and we spent most of that time in Aedan's cabin. Which is now my cabin, too. His crew - my crew - got used to having to deal with things without their captain. Aedan has shown me pleasures I never thought possible. I never thought of myself as a nymphomaniac - on the opposite - but this male has turned me into a constantly horny female willing to jump him all day. Or be jumped.

Professor Katila has backed off and the cameras have been removed. Len went through the ship searching for hidden bugs. Aedan got so angry I had to resort to the only method that calms him down when he gets in one of his don't-look-at-my-mate moods: caressing his horns.

Len and Panan have become my friends, or at least are on the way to be. The brothers are easy to talk to and Panan has a wicked sense of humour. The other female on board, La-Layna, is a different story altogether. I don't know if she's jealous or simply doesn't like me, but we've come to something of a truce. We ignore each other most of the time and stay civil when we can't. Aedan says she'll need some time to get used to the idea of having me on board. The crew is La-Layna's family and having someone invade that dynamic must be difficult. I get that.

"What are you waiting for?" Aedan shouts and I realise I've been standing there lost in thought. I smile and join him on the blanket. Even the fabric is alien, unlike anything I've ever felt before. It's soft to sit on yet I don't feel the ground through it. I bet we could sit on rough stones without feeling them.

Aedan opens one of the plastic-like tubs and presents my favourite alien food: dumplings filled with something close to spinach. He takes one of them and holds it to my lips. I grin and open my mouth, letting him feed me. The dough melts in my mouth and I can't help but moan as the flavours explode in my mouth.

"I thought that sound was reserved for me," Aedan grins and strokes my bottom lip with his thumb. He knows how that drives me crazy.

"Give me another one of those dumplings and you can hear it again."

"I don't think so. Let's see if I can make you moan without relying on treats."

He cups my face and pulls me closer until our lips are only a breath apart.

"I love you, my mate," he whispers before crushing his lips against mine. He kisses me as if there's no tomorrow, claiming me, worshipping me. I forget all about the dumplings, the picnic, even the beautiful planet we're on.

All that matters is Aedan, his lips, his body.

He's mine. We're made for each other. And we'll stay together, forever, travelling the galaxy.

. . .

LATER, we're spooning on the blanket. His large body is wrapped around me, protecting me from the evening chill. The air now smells of roasted chestnuts and I breathe in deep.

"I can't believe we're here," I whisper. "How is this even possible? How did we end up together? In all of the universe, how did we find each other?"

"I would have always found you," Aedan replies. There's no doubt in his voice. "We're mates. Nothing in the galaxy could keep us apart. If I hadn't been caught, hadn't been forced to abduct you, I'm sure I would have one day travelled to Peritus and met you. The universe has a way of making sure destiny always wins. And you're my destiny, little human. You're my life. Always and forever."

"Always and forever," I repeat solemnly. "I love you, Aedan."

He hugs me tighter. "Say it again."

"I love you."

"I set out to abduct you," he whispers while stroking my hair. "But in the end, it was you who abducted my heart. You're a pirate and you don't even know it."

I chuckle. "You're such a romantic."

"I am. Don't tell anyone. And you know what I also am?"

"What?"

"A male who needs to make love to you."

A shiver runs down my back. These words...

I turn around. "I'm yours."

And then I kiss him and he kisses me and we

become one like we were meant to be. With all the stars as our witnesses.

THE END

Want more alien abduction lessons? Enrol at the IGU and read *Alien Abduction for Beginners*, a reverse harem featuring three hunky yet clueless aliens and the human woman they abduct.

Do you think you've got what it takes to become an alien abductor? Read on to take the test!

Don't want to miss a new release? Subscribe to my newsletter to get a free book: **skyemackinnon.com/newsletter**

COULD YOU ABDUCT A HUMAN?

Do you think you've got what it takes to become an alien abductor? Take this test to find out!
skyemackinnon.com/alien-abduction-test

(if you share your results on social media, be sure to tag me)

And if you feel like you've passed this course, you can download a certificate!
hi.switchy.io/AAFBcertificate

THE INTERGALACTIC GUIDE TO HUMANS

Abductions aren't easy - which is exactly why the Intergalactic University offers a range of courses at various levels. Immerse yourself in this strange, comical universe and work on your abduction skills.

Find all books in this series here:

skyemackinnon.com/intergalactic-guide

Alien Abduction for Beginners

Alien Abduction for Professionals

Alien Abduction for Experts

(*reverse harem/why choose trilogy, to be read in order*)

Alien Abduction for Santa

(*fmf standalone*)

Alien Abduction for Pirates

(*mf standalone*)

Alien Abduction for Milkmen

(*mm standalone*)

Alien Abduction for Unicorns

(*mf standalone*)

THE STARLIGHT UNIVERSE

This book is part of the Starlight Universe, an entire galaxy filled with hunky aliens, exotic planets, and the human women ready to find love among the stars.

Starlight Highlanders Mail Order Brides

Alien Highlanders in kilts come to Earth in search of brides... and take them to planet Albya. Three m/f standalones full of humour, action and steamy romance. Part of the Intergalactic Dating Agency.

The Intergalactic Guide to Humans

A humorous take on alien abductions, probing and other shenanigans. One reverse harem trilogy about clueless aliens and the human woman they abducted, followed by several standalone romances with various pairings (m/f, f/m/f and m/m). If you want light entertainment filled with unicorns, fabulous misunderstandings and unusual body parts, this is the series for you.

Starlight Vikings

Set on Earth and on the spaceship Valkyr, this trilogy of m/f standalones is all about hunky alien Vikings in need of females. Part of the Intergalactic Dating Agency.

Starlight Monsters

These aliens are not your usual humanoids... they have claws, fangs, tails, scales, knotty dicks and will growl at you. Interconnected m/f standalones with lots of action, steam and fated mates.

ABOUT THE AUTHOR

Skye MacKinnon is a Scottish romance author who was raised by elves in the mystical Highlands and calls the Loch Ness monster her friend. Her bestselling books weave together romance with action, suspense and whimsical humour, creating page-turners filled with strong heroines, alpha heroes and loveable monsters.

Whether she's writing about aliens in kilts, hunky Vikings or cat shifter assassins, Skye likes to put a new spin on familiar tropes. Some of her heroines don't have to choose, some fall in love with other women, and others get abducted by clueless aliens.

Skye lives with her bossy cat on the west coast of Scotland and uses the dramatic views from her office as an inspiration, no matter whether she writes fantasy, paranormal or science fiction romance. Until she gets abducted by aliens, that is.

Subscribe to her newsletter:

skyemackinnon.com/newsletter

ALSO BY SKYE MACKINNON

Find all of Skye's books on her website, skyemackinnon.com, where you can also order signed paperbacks and swag. Many of her books are available as audiobooks.

PARANORMAL & FANTASY ROMANCE

- **Claiming Her Bears** (post-apocalyptic shifter reverse harem)
- **Daughter of Winter** (fantasy reverse harem)
- **Catnip Assassins** (urban fantasy reverse harem)
- **Infernal Descent** (paranormal reverse harem based on Dante's Inferno, co-written with Bea Paige)
- **Seven Wardens** (fantasy reverse harem co-written with Laura Greenwood)
- **The Lost Siren** (post-apocalyptic, paranormal reverse harem co-written with Liza Street)

SCIENCE FICTION ROMANCE

- **Starlight Highlanders Mail Order Brides** (sci-fi m/f romance, part of the Intergalactic Dating Agency)
- **Starlight Vikings** (sci-fi m/f romance, part of the Intergalactic Dating Agency)
- **Starlight Monsters** (m/f romance)
- **The Intergalactic Guide to Humans** (sci-fi romance with various pairings)
- **Between Rebels** (sci-fi reverse harem set in the Planet Athion shared world)
- **The Mars Diaries** (sci-fi reverse harem)
- **Through the Gates** (dystopian reverse harem co-written with Rebecca Royce)
- **Aliens and Animals** (f/f sci-fi romance co-written with Arizona Tape)

OTHER SERIES

- **Academy of Time** (time travel academy standalones, reverse harem and m/f)
- **Defiance** (contemporary reverse harem with a hint of thriller/suspense)

STANDALONES

- Song of Souls – m/f fantasy romance, fairy tale retelling
- Wings of Time and Fate - YA fantasy

- Their Hybrid – steampunk reverse harem
- Partridge in the P.E.A.R. - sci-fi reverse harem co-written with Arizona Tape
- Highland Butterflies – lesbian romance

BOX SETS

- Daggers & Destiny – a Skye MacKinnon starter library
- Stars & Seduction - a Sci-Fi Romance starter library

www.ingramcontent.com/pod-product-compliance
Ingram Content Group UK Ltd.
Pitfield, Milton Keynes, MK11 3LW, UK
UKHW040011200726
13854UKWH00001B/149